Maggie Sinclair,

will you please fix your hair?!

A story by Hilary Grant Dixon

Illustrated by Gabrielle Howell

for Morgan, Coever, and Vivian, who love stories,
and for Gram, who inspired me to write this one,
and for Craig, who heard it first and smiled.

ISBN-13: 978-0-9905958-0-9

Gram comes to stay with me and Little Brother when Mom and Dad go away.

She does all of the things that Mom and Dad do: helps with homework, serves veggies, and plans trips to the zoo.

She even plays games, gives baths and tucks us in at night. But there's one thing that I just won't let Gram do: my hair! When she pulls out a brush, I duck out of sight!

Monday

A school day, so we're up with the sun. We have breakfast, get dressed, brush our teeth and we're done!

"Not so fast," says Gram, giving me a pointed stare. "Maggie Sinclair, will you *please* fix your hair?!"

"I did, Gram," I say, giving my head a shake. "I'm an Egyptian queen. See my crown with the coiling snake? I am overseeing my empire.

My *braids* shine with oil.
My silvery headpiece only looks like tinfoil! It sits atop my carefully-styled hair, just like all beautiful royal ladies wear."

Gram purses her lips and puffs out a sigh. "I suppose," she says, offering my lunch with a sweet kiss goodbye.

Tuesday

A rainy day: boots and slickers, puddles and clouds.
I'm still so very sleepy. My yawns are so very loud.

From down in the kitchen, I hear Gram declare,
"Maggie Sinclair, will you *please* fix your hair?!"

"I did, Gram," I say. "I have long, ropy *locs.*

I'm all four elements combined! Don't look so shocked. These locs are thick like fog and strong like thunder. My locs zigzag like lightning. Aren't they a wonder?"

Gram hands me an umbrella, her grin twitchy as a mouse. She says, "C'mon, young lady, before you blow the roof off the house."

Wednesday

Oooh, class picture day! My outfit is pressed, my smile perfected.
For some strange reason, Gram thinks my hair looks neglected.

I think I know what's coming. It almost sounds like a dare:
"Maggie Sinclair, will you *please* fix your hair?!"

"I did, Gram," I say with a satisfied smile.

I pat my *cornrows*, tight to my scalp in a '70s style.

The beads on the ends click and clack, beating out a
rhythm: *I am proud to be Black.* I twist this way and that;
I shimmy and shake. I swing them around 'til Gram
warns that my neck might break!

As I hustle outside, she
runs her hand over my
hair, tender and slow.
"Such a lovely design,"
she murmurs. "These
are pretty, you know."

Thursday

It's almost the weekend. Soon, Mom and Dad will be home. Little Brother's in my room trying to make it his own. Sometimes, he can be so *naughty*.

Hey! That gives me an idea.

Gram is up the stairs in a flash, as if my thoughts she can hear.
"Maggie Sinclair, will you please fix your hair?!"

"I did, Gram," I say, drawing myself up to my full height.
"I sectioned and moisturized all through the night.

These are *bantu knots,* tightly coiled, and well-kempt.

It didn't take long to do. They came out great on my first attempt!"

"I see," says Gram, giving my knots a pat.
She hands me my coat and my bag, and that's that.

friday

Mom and Dad are coming home today! What a week this has been. I hope Gram had fun and will come back again. Before she goes, she's sure to ask about my hair, but I've got a good answer. I'm extremely prepared.

"Maggie Sinclair, will you please fix your hair?!" comes the familiar refrain. "Come up and see, Gram," I call, patting my curly mane.

"Oh my!" Gram says, casting her eyes on the photo in my hand. A photo of a girl with hair extra big! It's little girl Gram!

"Would you look at that," Gram says with a smile.
"You look just like me! How did I miss *that* all the while?"

"I found this in Mom's room while looking for a bow. I stared at the face
and thought, 'This is someone I know!'

Your *curls* are wonderful, a halo around your face.
They look healthy, and soft, not a one out of place. You ask me to fix
my hair, but Gram, don't you see? My hair looks like *yours,* in this picture
especially. It's not broken or messy. There's no fixing to do. I love my
hair, Gram. I got it from you."

That night, Mom and Dad were in for a treat. Showered with hugs, our family was reunited and complete.

At bedtime, I asked for one more tuck-in from Gram. She came into my room, the framed picture in her hand.

"Thank you, Miss Maggie," she began with a wink. "Spending time with you has really made me think. I'd forgotten all the wonderful things that my hair can do. You're right, it doesn't need fixing. I know now that's true. Sweet Maggie Mae," Gram went on, "we make quite a pair. Thank you, my sweetheart, for loving this hair."

She gave me a kiss on the top of my head, made sure my bonnet was in place and tucked me into bed. Gram clicked out the light, and as she shut the door with care, she turned back to say, "Maggie Sinclair, thanks for reminding me to love my own hair!"

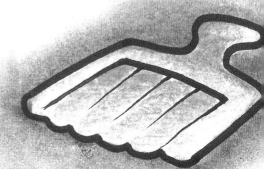

Maggie Sinclair

Let's Learn About Hair!

Braids

Ancient Egyptians often shaved their heads to keep cool. They wore elaborately braided wigs as headdresses, topped with cones of scented wax, which would release fragrance as it melted in the warm climate. The rearing cobra, or Ureus, was used as a symbol of royalty and divine authority in ancient Egypt.

Dreadlocks

Dreadlocks (or dreds, dreads, locs, locks), are matted coils of hair, formed by allowing the hair to grow in tangled, twisted ropes when left to its own devices. This intentional method, referred to as organic free form, is the mostly widely known. Most commonly associated with the Rastafari movement, individuals from ethnic groups across the globe wear locs for religious, cultural or stylistic reasons.

Cornrows

Cornrows are a form of hairstyling in which the hair is picked up and gathered along a row to form tight braids against the scalp. A way of styling hair that can be traced to North Africa, East Africa, and West Asia, cornrows, or rows, are created by sectioning the hair and braiding the hair in an underhand, upward motion.

Bantu Knots

Also referred to as Zulu knots, this hairstyle originated from the Bantu group of West Africans. Bantu Knots can be achieved with long or short hair and became popular due to its ability to manage unruly, wayward hair.

Afro

Afro, or 'fro or natural, is a hairstyle worn naturally by people with kinky, spring-like hair. It is created without the assistance of hot combs, flat irons or chemicals. Instead, wearers use a wide tooth comb, or pick, to extend the hair away from the scalp. In so doing, the hair forms a large, rounded shape, much like a ball or halo.

For more information about any of these hairstyles, email Hilary at hilary@hilarygrantdixon.com

About the Author

Hilary Grant Dixon is a writer, photographer and award winning creative genius. A curly girl who began her natural hair journey over fourteen years ago, she is as well known for her hair as she is for her honest, thoughtful style of writing on her blog, *Hilary With One L.* Hilary lives in Richmond, Virginia with her husband and three curly girlies.

Maggie Sinclair, Will You Please Fix Your Hair?! is her first book.

35166518R00020

Made in the USA
Lexington, KY
01 September 2014